Saved By The Master Sergeant

The Brotherhood, Volume 1

Mia Caldwell and Mylia Ashton

Published by Mia Caldwell, 2023.

Blurb

She walked into his bar and straight into his heart...

WHEN KINSEY STUMBLES into his bar, fleeing her abusive ex-boyfriend, Sawyers latent protective instincts stir to life. He thought he left that behind when an IED forced him to retire from the Rangers, but she makes him want to protect and cherish her. Taking her to his friend's ranch is the best way he knows to protect her as he waits for his former unit to join them. They've all been torn up by the same IED, in more ways than one, but with Kinsey, Sawyer sees a chance to start to heal. Kinsey feels safe with him, and he'll do anything to protect her.

This is a steamy, age gap BWWM romance.

Chapter 1

KINSEY HAD BEEN RUNNING for what felt like hours. Her ex-boyfriend, Jake, had gone completely off the rails, and he was determined to track her down. She had no idea how he had found her, but she knew she couldn't go home. So she kept running until she saw the neon sign for a bar and ducked inside.

The bartender looked up from the glass he was cleaning as Kinsey rushed in. "We're closed, and you're too young..." He trailed off after looking more closely at her. "You're shaking like a leaf. What's going on?" His voice was low and soothing.

Kinsey took a deep breath and tried to calm herself. "My ex-boyfriend is after me," she said, her voice shaking. "He attacked me, and I had to run."

"You're safe here. No one's going to hurt you." He reached under the bar to remove a handgun. "Name's Sawyer, and this is my place."

Kinsey breathed a sigh of relief and sank onto one of the barstools. Sawyer moved down the counter to where she was sitting and poured her a glass of water. "Here," he said, sliding it toward her. "Drink this."

Kinsey took a sip and then another. The cool liquid helped soothe her frayed nerves. She looked up at Sawyer, who was watching her closely. There was something in his gaze that made her heart skip a beat. It was as though he saw right through her, to the scared and vulnerable person she was inside.

She had never been so scared in her life. She had thought Jake loved her, but now she saw he was capable of real violence. Kinsey's heart pounded in her chest as she spoke to Sawyer, her voice barely above a whisper. She had never been so scared in her life. "He... he hit me," she said, her hands shaking. "He...he was angry, and he started yelling, and then he just...he hit me." She touched her stomach, slowly lifting the shirt to see if she had a bruise. The skin was unmarred, thankfully, so she doubted she had to worry about internal bleeding.

Sawyer's face darkened with anger, and he took her hand. "I'm so sorry," he said, his voice rough with emotion.

"I just... I had to get away from him. I was so scared, and he came after me."

Sawyer's eyes narrowed as he listened to her story. "Has he hurt you before?"

Kinsey shook her head, tears welling. "He's always been possessive and controlling, but I never thought he would hurt me."

As she recounted the story of her ex-boyfriend and their tumultuous relationship, Sawyer listened intently. The anger in his eyes left her relieved that someone else understood just how terrible Jake had been.

"And now he's after you?" Sawyer asked, his voice low and intense.

Kinsey nodded, her voice shaking. "He's convinced that I'm his property. He thinks he can control me, and that I'll come back to him."

"Do you have any idea where he might be?" Sawyer asked.

She shook her head, feeling more hopeless than ever. "He could be anywhere. He's always been very secretive."

Sawyer was quiet for a moment, deep in thought. "We'll need to be careful," he said. "If he's as possessive as you say, he could be tracking you."

Kinsey's heart sank. She had heard Jake talk about the tracking and surveillance technology his father's company specialized in. She knew that Jake had access to it, and that he had used it to keep tabs on her in the past. "He's always been very tech-savvy," she said, feeling a lump form in her throat. "His father owns a tech company that specializes in tracking and surveillance. He's claimed he's used it to spy on me before."

Sawyer's expression grew serious. "We need to assume he could be tracking us at any moment," he said. "We'll have to be extra cautious."

"It's not your problem." She spoke the truth, feeling like she needed to admit that.

His expression gentled. "Maybe not, but I'm making it my problem, unless you don't want help?"

She shook her head. "I do. I just don't want to dump this all on a stranger. It's not your place to watch out for me."

"I'm making it my place for now. We'll figure it out," he said, taking her hand. "I won't let anything happen to you."

For the first time in hours, Kinsey felt like she might actually be able to relax, even if just a little bit. With Sawyer by her side, maybe she had a fighting chance.

Sawyer walked around the counter to put a hand on her shoulder. "Come with me. I have a back room where you can stay for the night."

Kinsey followed him, relieved to rely on someone else, even for a little while. He led her to the room and left her there on the couch. "I have to finish cashing out and closing, but I'll be back."

She nodded. "Thank you." As she settled into the back room, Kinsey thought about Sawyer. He was so kind and protective, and she found herself drawn to him in a way she couldn't quite explain. She was in no position to start a relationship, but she couldn't help but feel a spark of something between them.

He returned a short time later, bringing her a glass of soda and some mozzarella sticks. "Sorry. We don't have much of a menu."

She took it, glad to have any food, and started wolfing it down. Halfway through, she burst into tears.

He looked alarmed, but he seemed to want to cheer her up. "I know they aren't great, but are the sticks really that bad?"

She laughed/snorted as she regained control before she managed to speak again. "I don't know what to do next."

He sat down on the couch next to Kinsey and took her hand. The warmth of his skin against hers was reassuring, and comfort washed over her. As he spoke, his voice was low and steady, and Kinsey couldn't help but be drawn to him. He spoke with such certainty and confidence she found herself trusting him completely.

"Don't worry. We'll figure it out together. Right now, the most important thing is to keep you safe."

Kinsey nodded, feeling grateful for his reassurance. "Thank you." She managed to finish the greasy snack, washed down with the cola, before stretching out on the sofa at his insistence. She didn't expect to sleep, so it was a surprise to find herself drifting off moments later as Sawyer covered her with a blanket. She was aware of the quiet hum of a television as he turned it on, along with the soft glow of the TV illuminating the room, as she fell asleep.

Either minutes or hours later, she jolted awake to the sound of shouting. Her heart raced as she looked around, trying to figure out what was happening. Then she saw him: Jake, standing in the doorway, his eyes wild with anger.

"You stupid bitch. I can always find you." He shook his iPhone at her.

Kinsey's stomach dropped as she realized how he had found her. He must have been following her on Life360, the GPS app she had forgotten to turn off. She had been so careful, but one mistake was all it took. She wouldn't even have it on her phone if he hadn't put it on there and checked every few days to make sure she hadn't deleted it.

Jake's gaze locked onto hers, and she saw the rage and possessiveness in his gaze. "You thought you could run away from me?"

Sawyer stepped forward, positioning himself between Kinsey and Jake. "Get out. You're not welcome here."

Jake just laughed, his eyes flicking back to Kinsey. "I'm not leaving without her."

Kinsey trembled in terror. She'ad never seen Jake like this before. He was unhinged, dangerous, and coldly determined—a lethal combination. She needed to get away from him, but she didn't know how.

Sawyer stepped forward, his fists clenched at his sides. "You're not taking her anywhere."

"What's it to you?"

"I'm protecting her."

"She's mine. She doesn't need anyone to protect her from *me*." Jake lunged forward, and Kinsey screamed.

Sawyer's arms wrapped around her, pulling her out of the way as Jake barreled into the room. Glass broke as he crashed into a table, and then Sawyer's body tensed as he pushed her away gently and tackled Jake.

Kinsey scrambled to her feet, her heart pounding in her chest. Sawyer and Jake grappled on the ground, each trying to gain the upper hand. She should do something to help, but she was frozen in fear.

Finally, Sawyer managed to get the upper hand, pinning Jake to the ground. "Stay away from her," he snarled, his voice low and dangerous.

Jake's eyes narrowed, and Kinsey could saw the rage burning inside of him. "You can't protect her forever. She's mine, and I'll do whatever it takes to get her back."

With that, he pushed Sawyer off him and ran out of the room. Kinsey watched him go, her heart racing with fear and adrenaline. She had to get away from him, and she was grateful to have Sawyer by her side. A sense of relief washed over her, but it was quickly replaced by intense fear. Jake was dangerous, and he wouldn't stop until he had her back under his control.

Sawyer stood up, his chest heaving with exertion. "Are you okay?" he asked, his voice rough.

Kinsey nodded as her gaze moved to Sawyer's. She blinked back tears prompted by him risking his own safety to protect her. They stood there for a second, their gazes locked onto each other. Kinsey sensed the electricity between them. It was a spark of attraction that had been growing ever since they had met.

Finally, Sawyer broke the silence. "Come on. Let's get out of here."

Together, they hurried out of the bar and into Sawyer's car. Adrenaline still pumped through her veins, and she was shaking with fear and excitement.

As they drove away, Kinsey couldn't help staring at Sawyer. He was so brave, and so strong. She couldn't deny the way she already wanted him. She knew that was risky, especially with everything that was going on, but she couldn't help the way she felt.

As they pulled up to a hotel, Sawyer turned to her. "I don't want you to be alone tonight," he said. "We'll get a room and, I'll sleep on the second bed."

She didn't hesitate, not wanting to be alone and already certain she could rely on him. She felt safe with Sawyer, trusting him more than she had ever trusted anyone before.

Together, they got a room and went upstairs. It was a modest room with two beds, and Kinsey settled onto the bed farthest from the door. Sawyer took the other bed, but she could feel his presence there, and it was a comfort in the dark.

As she drifted off to sleep, Kinsey knew that things were far from over. She was afraid of Jake, and what he'd do, but it was easy to find strength in Sawyer's determination. He was a stranger, but she felt like she'd known him forever already.

Chapter 2

SAWYER WOKE UP EARLY the next morning, his mind still buzzing from the events of the night before. He couldn't stop thinking about Kinsey, and about how scared she must have been when Jake showed up at the bar.

He got up quietly, careful not to wake her, and headed to the office to claim their continental breakfast. As he returned with the two paper plates, he didn't try to pretend he wasn't drawn to her. He couldn't deny that, and the need to protect her and more, had roared to life when she burst into his bar last night. Even though they were in the middle of a dangerous situation, it couldn't dim his libido or automatic response as he let himself back into the room and saw the blanket had slipped enough to display the bra she slept in, along with the curvy breasts beneath.

He was determined to protect her. He couldn't control what happened in the outside world, but he could make sure she was safe and taken care of while she was with him. That included not being ogled in her sleep, so he wrenched his gaze from her as he set down the plates.

She started to stir, and he said, "Breakfast."

Kinsey lifted her head, looking a little disoriented. "Good morning," she said, her voice groggy.

Sawyer smiled at her. "Good morning," he said. "I got breakfast."

Kinsey's eyes lit up. "Wow. You didn't have to do that."

Sawyer shrugged. "I wanted to, and it's included with the rate." He waved his hand at the plates. "It's nothing special. Just rolls and some crumbled scrambled eggs that look a lot like that dehydrated crap they served us in Afghanistan."

She got up and came to sit with him at the scarred table with its two mismatched chairs. "My stomach doesn't care."

"Your tastebuds might," he warned with a grin as he held out a chair for her before taking the one beside her.

They sat together and ate in comfortable silence. Her nose curled at the first bite, but she kept eating.

Sawyer couldn't help but steal glances at Kinsey as she ate, taking in the way that her hair fell in tight black curls around her warm brown face, and the way her brown eyes sparkled in the morning light. He wanted to tell her how beautiful she was, but the words stuck in his throat. He was too old, bitter, and scarred for someone so young and innocent.

"I don't know what to do or how to handle this." She whispered that as she pushed away her empty plate.

"Do you have family or friends you can turn to?"

She hesitated and then shook her head. "My mother and I aren't close. I left home at seventeen to avoid her latest boyfriend. I've been working at a restaurant and had some work friends, but Jake cut me off from all of them over the months we were together. We were never close enough that they'd want to risk themselves for me."

Sawyer's heart ached for Kinsey as he listened to her story. He couldn't imagine what it must have been like to be so isolated. He wanted to wrap her in his arms and protect her from the world, to make her feel safe and loved, but he couldn't do that. Not yet, at least. They were still in the middle of a dangerous situation, and he needed to keep a clear head if he was going to protect her.

"Okay. We'll figure it out. For now, let's just focus on staying safe."

Kinsey nodded, and they spent the rest of the day holed up in the hotel room, trying to stay calm and avoid drawing attention to themselves. She seemed lost in thought, and he didn't want to disturb her. He wasn't much of a conversationalist anyway, so he was content with the silence.

As the day slipped into night, a sense of unease crept over him. Jake was still out there and still hunting for Kinsey. He had to be prepared for whatever came their way. As a former Ranger, he should be prepared, but it had been a while since that IED forced his retirement. He was nervous about keeping her safe.

Realizing he didn't have to do this alone, he waited until she'd fallen asleep on her bed before getting out his cellphone. He spent the next hour making calls to his former Army buddies, explaining the situation and asking for their help. He called Mike first, who lived in Chicago. They talked on the phone for a while, discussing their plan of action.

"We need to keep her safe," said Mike. "We can't let this guy get anywhere near her."

"I've got her here in a hotel room for now, but we need a more secure location. I was thinking we could all meet up at Cooper's ranch in Texas. It's isolated and secure." Cooper had dropped off the grid since the IED that retired their little unit. "Do you think he'll agree?"

"Great idea. I think he'll agree, even if he doesn't want people around. He's still a Ranger in his heart, just like the rest of us." They made plans to meet up in Texas in a few days unless Cooper vetoed the plan, which was unlikely.

Next, Sawyer called their former communication officer, Viper (real name: Vance, but he liked to go by his old handle), who also lived in Chicago. Viper picked up on the second ring. "Sawyer, my man. What's up?"

Sawyer quickly filled him in on the situation with Kinsey and Jake. "We're trying to come up with a plan to keep her safe," he said. "I was hoping you could come down to Texas and help us out."

"Of course, bro," said Viper. "Anything for you. I'll be there as soon as I can."

Sawyer breathed a sigh of relief. With Mike and Viper on board, plus Cooper, they would have a solid team to protect Kinsey. "Thanks, Viper. I knew I could count on you."

"Hey, that's what brothers are for," said Viper, his voice serious.

After hanging up with Viper, Sawyer made one more call. He hesitated for a moment before dialing the number, feeling a sense of guilt and shame for even considering involving him in this mess.

The phone rang several times before a gruff voice answered. "What do you want, Sawyer?"

Sawyer took a deep breath. "Cooper, I need your help. I know we haven't talked in a while, but I don't know who else to turn to." There was a long pause on the other end of the line. Sawyer could practically hear Cooper's skepticism.

"What's the situation?" asked Cooper finally.

Sawyer quickly filled him in, explaining about Kinsey and Jake and the danger they were in. "I need a secure location to keep her safe. I was hoping we could use your ranch."

Cooper was quiet for a moment before answering. "I don't know, Sawyer. I've been trying to stay off the grid for a reason."

"I know." His friend's mangled face was vivid in his memory. "I understand, but this is important. Kinsey's life is in danger. I wouldn't ask if it wasn't serious."

There was another long pause before Cooper finally sighed. "Fine, but you owe me one."

Sawyer breathed a sigh of relief. "Thanks, Cooper. I mean it."

"See you in a few days," said Cooper, and hung up.

Sawyer was relieved as he hung up the phone. With the help of his old Ranger unit, he could keep Kinsey safe. He was determined to do whatever it took to protect her, no matter what.

Realizing it was a little past dawn, and he still hadn't slept, he finally dropped onto the unoccupied hotel bed and stretched out. He slept lightly, but after years of nightmares, any sleep was appreciated.

Chapter 3

KINSEY WOKE TO THE sound of rustling as Sawyer shifted in his sleep. She looked over and saw him sleeping peacefully in the bed beside hers. For a moment, she just watched him, taking in the way his chest rose and fell with each breath. His skin was had a healthy tanned glow, and his blond hair was like a halo around his head. She tried not to pigeonhole her interest in men, but he was the first blond she'd been attracted to, though it suited him. His blue eyes, when they opened, were gorgeous with his skin and hair.

She fanned herself, feeling flushed as she thought about what he looked like under the sheet covering him. Her experience was limited, since Jake had been her only lover, and he was on the thin side, with sharp angles that didn't feel like bulging muscles.

She cleared her throat and jerked away her gaze, feeling like a pervert as she admired his sleeping form.

As she started to get up, Sawyer's eyes opened, and he sat up quickly. "Are you okay?" he asked, looking concerned.

Kinsey nodded, feeling a little embarrassed for waking him up. "Sorry, I didn't mean to startle you."

Sawyer rubbed his eyes and yawned. "It's okay. I should probably get up anyway."

He stood up and stretched, and Kinsey couldn't help but admire the way his muscles bulged beneath his shirt. She quickly looked away, feeling a flush rise to her cheeks.

Sawyer turned back to her and sat down on the bed. "I talked to my buddies last night. We're going to meet up at my friend's ranch in Texas. It's secluded and secure, so we'll be able to keep you safe."

Kinsey nodded, relieved. "Thank you, but is it going to cost anything? I don't have much money."

Sawyer shook his head. "Don't worry about that. We've got it covered. The most important thing is keeping you safe."

Kinsey felt grateful for his kindness, but also a little guilty for being a burden on him and his friends. She needed their help, but she didn't like feeling helpless.

Sawyer seemed to sense her unease and reached over to take her hand. "Don't worry. We're in this together, and we'll figure it out."

Kinsey nodded, feeling a little better. She trusted Sawyer and his friends, and they would do everything in their power to protect her. "So, what's the plan?"

Sawyer stood up and started to gather his things. "We need to get some supplies and then get out of the city. We don't want to risk Jake finding us. We'll start driving toward Texas and make a few stops along the way to rest and stock up on food and other supplies."

Kinsey nodded, scared. They were taking a risk by staying in one place for too long. Jake was smart and resourceful, and she didn't doubt he would stop at nothing to find her. She trembled.

Sawyer must have noticed because he touched her shoulder and spoke gently. "We'll be careful, and we won't take any unnecessary risks."

Kinsey nodded, grateful for his reassurance. "Okay. What can I do to help?"

Sawyer looked at her, considering. "Right now, you should just focus on resting and staying safe, but once we're on the road, there might be things you can help with. Like keeping an eye out for anything suspicious or helping with navigation."

Kinsey nodded, glad she would have a role to play. She didn't want to be a burden on Sawyer and his friends, and she was determined to do whatever she could to help.

Sawyer finished packing up his things and turned to her. "Are you ready to go?"

Kinsey nodded as nervous excitement washed over her. She didn't know what the future held, but with Sawyer by her side, she was less afraid.

They hit the road and drove for a few hours, stopping every now and then to rest and stock up on supplies. Kinsey did her best to help, keeping an eye out for anything suspicious and helping with navigation. Sawyer seemed tense, his eyes darting around as if he was searching for something.

After about an hour of driving, Sawyer suddenly became tenser. Kinsey could feel the tension in the air, and she finally asked, "What's wrong?"

Sawyer hesitated for a few seconds before finally speaking. "I think we're being followed."

Kinsey's heart raced as she looked around, trying to spot whoever was following them. "Are you sure?"

Sawyer nodded. "I saw a car that looked like it was following us," he said. "It's been behind us for a while now."

Kinsey trembled. "What do we do?"

Sawyer seemed to consider it for a moment before finally speaking. "We need to lose them," he said. "We'll take a few turns and see if they keep following us. If they do, we'll try to lose them on the highway."

Kinsey nodded, tensing as he started to drive more erratically. They were in a dangerous situation, but she trusted Sawyer to keep her safe. He continued driving, taking turns and making sudden stops to try to lose their pursuer.

After a few tense minutes, they finally lost the car that had been following them. Sawyer let out a sigh of relief and pulled over to the side of the road. "We should be safe for now."

"How did he find us?"

Sawyer looked over at Kinsey, his expression grim. "I'm not sure, but my guess is he's using some kind of tracking technology."

Sawyer pulled back onto the road, and they continued driving in silence for a few minutes. Kinsey's mind was racing with thoughts of how Jake could be tracking her, and she couldn't help feeling a sense of paranoia.

Finally, Sawyer spoke up. "I think we should stop at the next big box store and get some burner phones. We can use those instead of our regular phones. And we should take the batteries out of our regular phones just to be safe."

Kinsey nodded, feeling grateful for his quick thinking. "That's a good idea. Do you think it'll work?"

Sawyer shrugged. "It's not foolproof, but it's better than nothing, and we need to do everything we can to throw Jake off our trail."

They continued driving, and after a few miles, they saw a Walmart coming up on the right. Sawyer pulled into the parking lot and parked the car. "Stay here. I'll be back in a few minutes."

Kinsey nodded and watched as he got out of the car and disappeared into the store. She tried to relax, but her heart was pounding with nervous energy. She couldn't shake the feeling they were being watched, and she couldn't wait to get out of the city and onto the open road.

Finally, Sawyer came back out with two new phones. "Let's do this," he said, and they removed the batteries from their real phones and set up the burner phones.

As they drove away from the Walmart, Kinsey was relieved. They weren't out of the woods yet, but she felt a little safer with the burner phones and their regular phones currently disabled. As they continued driving, the tension between Kinsey and Sawyer started to ease. They chatted about small things, trying to distract themselves from the danger they were in.

After several hours, they finally pulled into a hotel parking lot. Sawyer parked the car and turned to Kinsey. "You go ahead and take the first shower," he said. "I'm going to examine the perimeter and bring in my rifle. I want to make sure we're safe."

Kinsey nodded, feeling a little nervous again. She grabbed her bag and headed into the hotel room. Once inside, she locked the door and started to relax. She was grateful for the chance to clean up and rest for a little bit.

As she showered, she couldn't help but think about Sawyer. She trusted him completely and was grateful for everything he was doing to keep her safe, but there was far more to it than that. She was starting to feel something for him, but she tried to push those thoughts aside. She couldn't afford to let herself get distracted.

When she finished her shower, she wrapped herself in a towel and stepped out of the bathroom. Sawyer was sitting on the bed, cleaning his rifle. He looked up as she entered the room and gave her a reassuring smile. "Feeling better?"

Kinsey nodded, grateful for the hot shower. "Thank you."

Sawyer set down the rifle and stood up. "I'm going to take a quick shower myself, and then we can figure out our next move."

Kinsey nodded and sat down on the bed. As she waited for Sawyer to finish, she couldn't help but think about how much she relied on him. He was her protector, her ally, and her friend. She didn't know what she would do without him.

She hated that for a moment. Not that she needed him, but that he didn't realize exactly how much she needed him. It wasn't just to keep her safe. She wanted so much more from Sawyer, but how to show him that?

Chapter 4

SAWYER HAD FINISHED his shower quickly, eager to get back to Kinsey. He had no idea what to expect when he stepped out of the bathroom, but he certainly hadn't been expecting this. Kinsey, who moments before had been deep in thought, seeming heartbreakingly lost, now sat with her towel draped over the hotel chair, leaving her naked.

"What are you doing?" The question sounded more like an accusation.

She flinched and licked her lips. "I wanted to thank you for protecting me," she said, her voice just a whisper.

He scowled. "I don't expect you to fuck me for helping you. Get dressed."

Her lower lip wobbled, and he expected her to reach for the towel. Instead, she stood up and came closer, reaching for his towel even as her hand shook. "It's not about that. I want you, Sawyer. Not because of what you're doing for me, but because I want you...this."

He stepped closer to her and for a moment, all he could focus on was her. Her brown skin was warm and inviting, her plump lips formed a bumper for a deep and alluring smile, and the tips of her nipples, a nut-brown, stood erect as though begging for his touch. Sawyer didn't understand why she would be thanking him like this, why she would be offering herself to him, but in spite of all his doubts and confusion, he didn't say no.

He knelt beside her, and she reached out to take his hand. She ran her fingertips across his palm as she spoke, her voice teasing and inviting.

"I want you," she said. "I want to show you much I care about you."

Sawyer felt the heat of her words wash over him with the sudden realization that she wanted him, just as he wanted her. He allowed himself to be swept away in the moment, aware of the pounding of his heart and the sweet scent of her skin.

Kinsey moved closer to him, her eyes searching his as if she could read his every thought.

A wave of desire washed over him along with an answering warmth inside. "Baby, I want you, but you have to know about my scars."

Sawyer took a deep breath, his eyes flickering down to the scars crisscrossing his skin as he lowered his towel. He had never let anyone see them before besides his unit and doctors, but Kinsey deserved to see the truth. "During my last tour in Afghanistan, I was hit by an IED," he said, his voice low and tight. "It left me with these scars."

Kinsey's eyes widened in shock, but she didn't recoil. Instead, she reached out to touch the jagged lines of his scars, tracing them with her fingertips. "They're part of you," she said softly. "I accept all of you, Sawyer. Scars and all."

Sawyer felt a lump form in his throat as he looked down into her beautiful brown eyes. He had never felt so vulnerable or exposed. Yet he was also relieved to know Kinsey accepted him for who he was. For the first time in a long time, Sawyer felt like he had found something worth fighting for, and he was willing to do whatever it took to keep Kinsey safe and by his side.

He leaned in and pressed his lips to hers, pouring all his emotions into the kiss. Kinsey responded eagerly, her hands roaming over his skin to trace the contours of his muscles. Sawyer deepened the kiss, pulling her closer until their bodies were pressed together.

The kiss lengthened, an electric fusion filled with unspoken emotion. He felt himself surrendering to her touch, to the passion that swirled between them like an invisible force. His hands moved across her body, exploring every curve with relish.

She gasped against his mouth and leaned into him, her warmth radiating through every inch of his body. His control was slipping away, and he wanted nothing more than to give in completely. Kinsey's lips parted and their tongues met in a passionate embrace.

Sawyer deepened the kiss even further, letting his hands slip beneath the towel and onto her bare skin. She shivered beneath his touch and clutched at him as if she never wanted him to let go. Her fingers brushed against his chest, sending shockwaves of pleasure through him.

He pulled away from her for a moment, needing to catch his breath before he lost himself entirely. "Are you sure about this?"

Kinsey smiled up at him, looking both beautiful and vulnerable in that moment. "I've never been surer of anything."

With a sigh of relief, he brushed the hair from her face and cupped her chin gently in one hand before lowering his lips back to hers for another long kiss. This time there was no hesitation or holding back. It was pure blissful pleasure.

Kinsey's breathing grew deeper and faster as they explored each other with their hands and mouths. Sawyer grew more aroused by the second until he couldn't take it anymore. He needed to be inside of her right now or he thought he might go mad with desire. "I can't wait any longer."

He pulled away again just long enough to reach for a condom on the nightstand before lowering himself down on top of Kinsey on the bed below them. The feeling of sliding inside of her had never been so intense or so heavenly. It seemed almost too good to be true that this woman could make him feel so alive with just a kiss and a single touch...

Kinsey responded eagerly, her fingers wandering over his back and pulling him closer until there seemed to be no space between them. He let out a low moan as she moved her body against his, each touch setting his skin alive with pleasure.

Sawyer felt himself slipping away and welcomed it. His body was alive with pleasure. He was floating on air as Kinsey moved beneath him. Her touch was like a drug, and he wanted more of it. He wanted to lose himself in her completely.

He groaned deeply, his hips meeting hers eagerly as their lovemaking intensified. She cried out in pleasure and wrapped her legs around his waist, her fingernails digging into his back as they moved faster and faster together.

The pleasure was so intense that Sawyer thought he might never come down from this high. It seemed almost too good to be true that they could find such a perfect connection their first time together in bed. He wanted nothing more than to stay there forever, locked in Kinsey's embrace until the end of time.

Their bodies writhed together, sweat glistening on their skin in the dim light of the room. Sawyer's passion built and built until it was a raging inferno, an unstoppable force that consumed them both. His movements grew more frantic, with his breath coming in short gasps as he approached the edge. Sawyer's movements became erratic as he neared the brink of ecstasy. His body tensed and his muscles tightened as he surrendered to the overwhelming pleasure coursing through him. He let out a guttural moan, his hips slamming against Kinsey's as he spilled himself inside her.

Kinsey's body shook with the intensity of her own orgasm, her cries of pleasure echoing in the room. She clung to Sawyer, her nails digging into his skin as he continued to thrust into her, prolonging the pleasure. Finally, they collapsed onto the bed, their bodies slick with sweat as they basked in the afterglow.

Sawyer rolled over onto his back, pulling Kinsey with him so that she laid against on his chest.

"That was incredible." Her fingers traced lazy circles on his chest.

Sawyer smiled, his hand stroking her thick curls, which had become kinkier with air drying. He loved that. "You're incredible," he said, his voice full of emotion.

Sawyer laid there motionless, holding Kinsey tightly in his arms. His heart was still pounding, and his mind still filled with wonder at what had just happened between them. He had never felt this way before, so completely connected to another person.

He stared up at the ceiling, the swell of emotions almost too much for him to take in. He couldn't believe he'd finally found someone who made him feel alive and complete. Somehow Kinsey had managed to fill the voids in his life he hadn't even known were there until now.

He kissed the top of her head softly, silently thanking her for coming into his life. In that moment, he swore he would do whatever it took to keep her by his side forever.

After a few more moments of blissful contentment, Sawyer eventually drifted off into a deep sleep with Kinsey still in his arms—feeling safe and secure like never before.

Chapter 5

KINSEY WOKE IN HIS embrace, content with the way he held her and her decision to put herself out there and tell him she wanted him. She looked up at him and smiled, feeling happy about what had happened between them last night. Now that they were lovers, how would things change? "Good morning," she whispered.

Sawyer opened his eyes and smiled back at her. "Good morning. Did you sleep well?"

Kinsey nodded. "Yeah, I did. I'm really happy about last night."

Sawyer's smile widened. "Me too," he said, leaning in to kiss her.

They got up and started packing their things, getting ready to hit the road again. Kinsey was nervous as they headed out. Even though they had burner phones and were being careful, Jake was still out there, watching and waiting for his chance to strike.

They stopped for gas a few hours later, and Kinsey went inside to use the restroom. As she was washing her hands, she heard the door slam open behind her. She turned around and saw Jake standing there, a wild look in his eyes.

"Kinsey," he shouted, grabbing her arm. "You're coming with me."

Kinsey screamed and tried to pull away, but he was too strong. She heard footsteps running toward the bathroom before Sawyer burst in, his rifle in hand.

"Let her go, Jake," he said, his voice cold and steady.

Jake sneered at him but seemed wary of the rifle. "You can't stop me," he said, and then shoved Kinsey toward Sawyer and made a run for it.

Sawyer grabbed Kinsey and held her close, watching as Jake climbed into an SUV and drove away. "Dammit. He's still following us."

Panic consumed her. How could Jake still be following them? They had gotten rid of their phones and were being careful. "Do you have any idea how he's doing it?" she asked, her voice shaking.

Sawyer shook his head as he led her from the bathroom back to the car, keeping a protective arm around her waist. "I don't know, but we need to figure it out before he catches up to us again." He smiled after a moment. "I might know someone who can help us. My old commander, Clayton, now works in cybersecurity at Langley."

Once behind the wheel and back on the road, he pressed a button on the car's audio system to connect a call to Clayton. Kinsey heard the ringing on the other end, and then Clayton's voice came through the speakers.

"Sawyer, it's good to hear from you," said Clayton. "What's going on?"

Sawyer explained the situation with Jake and how he and his friends were trying to keep Kinsey safe. "We think he might be using some kind of tracking technology. Do you have any ideas on how he could be doing it?"

Clayton hesitated for a moment. "There are a few possibilities, but one thing you could do is check Kinsey for an RFID chip."

"An RFID chip?" asked Sawyer. "What's that?"

"It's a small, passive device that can be implanted under the skin and can be used for all sorts of things, like tracking pets or keeping track of inventory in a warehouse. If Jake has access to that kind of technology, he could have implanted one in Kinsey without her knowing."

"But how do we check for it?" asked Sawyer.

"You'll need a scanner," Clayton said. "You might be able to find one at a tech store or a large vet clinic. It shouldn't be too hard to use, but if you're not sure, I can talk you through it. Just call."

"Thanks, Clayton. I'll look into it."

"Good luck, and stay safe."

While Kinsey tried to absorb the thought that Jake might have tagged her like livestock, Sawyer drove to the next big city, stopping at a tech store. They approached the counter, and Sawyer asked the clerk if they had a scanner for RFID chips.

The clerk sneered at them. "What do you want that for?" he asked. "Trying to play spy games or something?"

Sawyer gritted his teeth, looking irritated. "It's not a game. We're trying to keep someone safe."

The clerk rolled his eyes. "Yeah, whatever. Try the CIA," he said, turning back to his computer screen.

Sawyer and Kinsey left the store feeling frustrated and defeated. As they walked through the strip mall, she spotted a large vet clinic across the way. "What about that clinic?"

He eyed it and nodded as they decided to try their luck there. They hurried across the parking lot and entered the clinic a moment later. It looked modern and clean, and it was likely to have state-of-the-art everything.

The receptionist at the vet clinic was clearly skeptical when Sawyer asked to use a scanner for an RFID chip. "I'm sorry, but we don't normally do that kind of thing."

Sawyer pulled out his wallet and slipped her a hundred-dollar bill. "Please. It's important."

The receptionist hesitated for a moment before nodding and showing them to an exam room. She brought in the scanner a moment later with a furtive air before slipping out.

Sawyer scanned Kinsey's body, and after a few tense moments, he let out a sigh. "There's a chip on the back of your neck. Jake must have implanted it in you without your knowledge."

Kinsey's eyes widened in shock and horror. "What? He put a chip in me? How could he do something like that without my knowledge?"

Sawyer's expression was grim. "I don't know, but we need to get it out of you. It's not safe to leave it there."

Outrage consumed her. "I can't believe he marked me like cattle," she said, her voice shaking. "I want it out. I'll cut it out myself if I have to." She was desperate to get it out of her, and not just because it allowed Jake to find her. He had no right to treat her like a thing.

Chapter 6

SAWYER SAW THE DESPERATION in Kinsey's eyes and knew she was serious about removing the chip herself if they couldn't find someone to do it for her. He took a deep breath and put on his most reassuring smile. "Hey, we'll find someone to take care of it. Don't worry."

"Now," she said with a hint of panic.

"Give me a minute." He ducked out of the room, scanning for any available personnel. The receptionist was busy answering phone calls, and the veterinarians must all be in the back, tending to their patients. He was getting despondent about finding someone there to help them, but then, he spotted a young woman in scrubs taking a break in the back corner of the waiting room.

He walked over to her and introduced himself. "Hey, I'm Sawyer. My friend needs some help, and we were wondering if you could assist us."

Emily cocked a brow. "With what? If your friend doesn't have four legs, it's not really my department." Sawyer explained the situation with the chip and Kinsey's urgent need to have it removed. Emily's expression softened, and she nodded. "Let me see if I can help. Follow me."

He took her back to the exam room where Kinsey waited. She was still visibly shaken and upset. He placed a reassuring hand on her shoulder and squeezed gently. "Emily is going to help us. She's a vet tech and can remove the chip for you."

Emily took a closer look at Kinsey's neck and nodded. "I see it. I can do this, but I'm not authorized to perform this kind of procedure, and Dr. Edson is currently in surgery."

Sawyer pulled out his wallet and slipped Emily a couple of hundred-dollar bills. "Please, we need your help. We can't wait for the doctor. We'll sign whatever waiver or release you need us to."

"I don't want this anywhere in writing." Emily hesitated for a moment before nodding and taking the money. "Okay, let's do this."

Sawyer could see the relief wash over Kinsey's face as Emily agreed to help. He knew how important it was to her to have the chip removed as soon as possible.

Emily pulled out a syringe and a vial of lidocaine. "I'm going to need to numb the area first," she said, calculating the amount she needed. "It's going to sting a little, but it shouldn't hurt too much."

Kinsey gritted her teeth as Emily injected the lidocaine into the area around the chip. Sawyer watched as Emily carefully worked to remove the chip from Kinsey's neck. Kinsey winced in pain even with the lidocaine, but Sawyer was there to hold her hand and reassure her. Fierce anger rose within him. How could Jake do something like this to her?

But he pushed the anger aside, focusing instead on being strong and steady for Kinsey. He knew she needed him to be her anchor in this storm.

Finally, after what felt like an eternity, Emily held up the tiny chip triumphantly. "Got it," she said as she turned to open a drawer.

Kinsey let out a sigh of relief, and Sawyer felt the tension draining from her body. He reached over and squeezed her hand. "You did great."

Emily handed them a small jar containing the chip. "Here you go. You might want to keep it as evidence in case you need it later."

Sawyer nodded, taking the jar from her. He felt a surge of anger and protectiveness toward Kinsey. Jake had gone too far, and Sawyer was determined to make sure he paid for what he'd done. For now, he focused on being strong and steady for Kinsey.

As they got back in the car, Sawyer handed Kinsey the jar with the chip. "Hang onto this."

Kinsey nodded, tucking the jar into her bag. "I can't believe he did something like that to me."

Sawyer's jaw clenched, and he tightened his grip on the steering wheel. "I know," he said, his voice tight with anger, "But we'll deal with him. Right now, we need to focus on keeping you safe."

They drove for hours, and the sun had begun to set by the time they finally reached Sweethome, Texas, passing right through it. They went another thirty miles to reach "EFF OFF Ranch." He chuckled at the name on the "welcoming" arch as they passed it.

Kinsey seemed apprehensive. "Do you think Cooper will let us stay?"

"Yeah. Don't take his ranch name to heart." Sawyer parked the car in front of the small house in the middle of sprawling land and turned to her, keeping his tone serious. "Just a heads up, but my friend Cooper has some scars from his time in the military. He's been through a lot, and I want you to be aware of that."

"What happened?"

He took a deep breath, the memory of their time in the military flooding back to him. "We were all injured in an IED explosion. Cooper took the brunt of it. He lost his leg, and we all sustained some serious injuries." Sawyer's voice trailed off, the pain of the memory still raw. "We were all medically discharged, either for physical or emotional wounds. It was a tough time for all of us."

He glanced over at Kinsey, hoping she understood the gravity of the situation. "Cooper's a good guy, but I just wanted to prepare you before we get there."

Kinsey nodded, her expression solemn. "Thank you for letting me know. I'll be respectful of his experiences."

Sawyer breathed a sigh of relief. She was strong and resilient, but these situations could be tough for anyone to handle. He was always slightly startled at seeing Cooper's ravaged face each time after a separation, so he imagined it would be hard for Kinsey, especially the first time. He was grateful to have her understand the gravity of the situation.

He had no reason to suspect she'd be cruel, even inadvertently, but he was still on edge as he grabbed their bags and led her to the front porch. A dog barked inside, and he shouted, "It's me, Scooter."

She smiled. "Scooter for a vicious dog?"

He snorted. "Sort of." As he answered, the door opened, and the Scottish terrier/mutt mix his friend had adopted leapt out, barking and growling at them. He held out his hand, reminding the dog of his scent. "You know me, Scooter."

The dog eased back, but he still seemed wary.

"Oh." She gasped, sounding frightened.

He thought she must have seen Cooper's face, but when he looked up, he saw Lex had followed his canine brother outside. Lex was a large mastiff mix and seemed ferocious. He'd been abandoned at the shelter because he was just too nice to be a guard dog, and Sawyer quickly told her that.

She took a step forward, holding out a hand. "Hello, Lex."

He thumped his tail and came closer, even as Scooter barked at her and whined at his brother, as if fearing the large dog was going to his death.

"He'll be fine," said a rough voice from inside the house, clearly addressing Scooter.

Sawyer recognized him immediately and stuck out his hand as Cooper edged outside. "It's good to see you."

Cooper sneered. "No one likes seeing me, but I'm glad you're here."

He was just as touchy as ever. Sawyer sighed, frustrated that his friend hadn't made much progress, but he couldn't really blame him. He turned to Kinsey, saying, "This is Cooper. He'll be our gracious host." His tone was only a little sarcastic, and he held his breath as he awaited Kinsey's reaction when she got her first full look at his friend's ruined face.

Chapter 7

KINSEY COULDN'T HELP but be startled by Cooper's appearance. His face was scarred and disfigured, and she could see the pain etched into his features, but she couldn't bring herself to pity him or act like she was afraid.

Instead, she took a deep breath and looked at him fully, maintaining eye contact as he welcomed them. "Thank you for letting us stay here," she said, her voice even and steady. "It's good to meet you."

Cooper grunted in response, but Kinsey could see a glimmer of surprise in his eyes. Sawyer had warned her about Cooper's scars, but seeing them up close was a different story. She was determined not to let it affect how she treated him though.

Cooper seemed momentarily taken aback by Kinsey's reaction, but he quickly composed himself and invited them inside. He led them to a small but cozy guest room, clearly assuming they were sharing, and left them to settle in.

After a few minutes, he knocked on the door and called out, "You guys settle in okay? Come on out and join me in the living room. Let's talk about what's happening."

Sawyer and Kinsey exchanged a look before following Cooper to the living room. The room was dimly lit, with a fire crackling in the fireplace. Cooper gestured for them to sit down on the couch, and he took a seat in a nearby armchair. "Okay, lay it out for me," he said, his voice gruff but not unkind. "What's going on?"

Kinsey took a deep breath before starting to tell Cooper what was happening. She explained everything, from the night she ran into Sawyer's bar to the moment they found the chip in her neck. She could see the anger in Cooper's face as she spoke, but he remained quiet until she finished.

"That's some heavy shit."

Kinsey nodded, feeling the weight of everything that had happened. "I know. It's been a nightmare."

Cooper looked at her for a long moment. "You stumbled into Sawyer's bar, huh?"

Kinsey nodded again, feeling a small smile tug at the corners of her mouth. "Yeah, it was the best thing that's happened to me in a while."

Cooper chuckled, and she could see some of the tension easing in his face. "He has a way of looking out for people. Always has."

She nodded. "He's been amazing. And so have you, letting us stay here."

Cooper shrugged, looking slightly uncomfortable with the praise. "We've all been through our fair share of shit, and I know what it's like to need a safe place to land."

They sat in silence for a moment before Cooper spoke up again. "So, what's the plan? How are we going to handle this?"

Kinsey took a deep breath, glad Cooper seemed to be taking their situation seriously. "Sawyer thinks we should hunker down and prepare for Jake to find us," she said. "We found the chip, but who knows what else he might have up his sleeve?"

Sawyer nodded, rubbing a hand over his face. "Yeah, he's not the kind of guy who gives up easily, but the cavalry's coming tomorrow."

Kinsey frowned in confusion. "What do you mean?"

Cooper leaned forward, his eyes intense. "Viper and Mike. They're flying in from Chicago tomorrow. We all served together, and they'll have our backs."

Kinsey was thrilled to have more people on their side. "That's great. What do we do in the meantime?"

Cooper sat back, looking thoughtful. "We fortify the ranch. Make sure we're prepared for anything. I've got supplies stockpiled, and we can set up a watch rotation. And we'll make sure you're trained in self-defense. Sawyer will handle that."

Kinsey felt a flicker of fear at the thought of having to defend herself, but it was necessary. "Okay. I'm willing to learn."

Sawyer nodded, looking satisfied. "Good. We'll get started tomorrow."

They retired a short time later, though Kinsey found it impossible to sleep. Her thoughts kept returning to the chip Jake had injected into her one night while she was sleeping. Her wound stung as if reminding her it was there, and her rage steadily grew. "I want him dead."

Sawyer didn't blink. "That might not be possible, but we are going to stop him."

Kinsey was exhausted, yet adrenaline coursed through her veins and pushed her mind into overdrive. She knew what she must do to protect herself but still felt that little spark of fear. She found it impossible to sleep. "I've never wanted anyone dead before." She felt no remorse for the wish.

"I understand, but you need to let it go tonight and rest." He leaned over to kiss her cheek. "Do you need a distraction?"

She turned her head, intrigued. "What kind of distraction?"

"This kind..." He trailed off as he started to kiss and stroke her.

Kinsey slowly relaxed as Sawyer's gentle caresses worked their magic on her restless mind. His touch was like a balm, soothing away her fears and replacing them with something else entirely. Her heart swelled with warmth and contentment as his lips roamed over her neck, sending little shivers of pleasure down her spine.

She gasped when he slid his hand between her legs, exploring her body even more. He moved slowly and carefully, as if he was trying to memorize every inch of her skin. Kinsey melted into the bed as she gave in to his touch, letting him take control.

Her breathing grew faster and deeper as he continued his exploration, and all thoughts of Jake's chip vanished from her mind. All that existed was the here and now—the feel of Sawyer's hands on her body, the smell of his cologne in the air, and the sound of his breath against her skin. Kinsey allowed herself to give in completely to his embrace, feeling safe and secure in his arms.

Sawyer's mouth soon followed his lips, and he took a deep breath before diving between her legs. Kinsey gasped as he began to work his magic, his tongue expertly exploring every inch of her. She grew more and more aroused with each passing moment, her body responding to his every touch.

Sawyer was relentless in his pursuit of her pleasure, teasing her and driving her wild with desire. Kinsey moaned and writhed beneath him, her hands clutching at the sheets as she surrendered herself to the waves of pleasure that washed over her.

As she reached the brink of orgasm, Sawyer slowed his pace, teasing her with a gentle touch before diving back in and sending her over the edge. Kinsey cried out his name as she came, her body shaking with the force of her release.

Sawyer kissed his way back up her body, pausing to nuzzle her neck before claiming her lips in a deep, passionate kiss. Kinsey melted into him once again, her body humming with pleasure and desire.

She held her breath as he finally entered her, feeling her entire body shiver with anticipation. He moved slowly and deliberately, building up the intensity until she was about to burst. His every move was sensual and expert, as if he had done this to her a thousand times before.

She gasped as he increased his pace, his thrusts becoming more urgent and intense. She was lost in the moment, her breathing heavy and ragged. She clung to him tightly, wanting nothing more than for him to never stop.

Finally, when Kinsey thought she could take no more pleasure from their lovemaking, Sawyer paused and looked deep into her eyes. She saw desire there—not just for her body but for something more—something Kinsey could only begin to comprehend. He moved his hips one final time, sending shock waves of pleasure through her body as he found his own release.

She screamed out his name in ecstasy as an orgasm of epic proportions washed over her being. Tears spilled from Kinsey's eyes as the intensity of it all threatened to overwhelm her senses. Sawyer slumped against her chest, taking a few moments to catch his breath before finally slipping off her and collapsing next to her on the bed.

Kinsey turned toward him and smiled, exhausted yet content in a way she had never experienced before. They simply laid in each other's arms until their breathing returned to normal, savoring every second they had together until they were ready to face reality once again.

Chapter 8

SAWYER WOKE EARLY THE next morning, feeling the warmth of Kinsey's body next to his. He smiled to himself, grateful for her presence, but they had to be prepared for the worst. He gently shook her awake.

"Good morning," he whispered, sitting up in bed. "We need to talk about some things before breakfast."

Kinsey groaned, pulling the covers up to her chin. "Can't we just eat first? I'm starving."

Sawyer shook his head. "We can't take any chances. You need to be prepared in case something happens. We're going to work on some self-defense moves, and you don't want to do that on a full stomach."

Kinsey's expression sobered as she sat up, rubbing the sleep from her eyes. "Okay," she said, nodding. "Let's do it."

Sawyer led her to the pasture out back and began to show her some basic self-defense moves. He showed her how to escape from a chokehold and how to defend herself against an attacker. He could see the fear in her eyes as they practiced, but he also saw determination that gave him hope.

They worked through the moves for what felt like hours, but in reality, it was only a few minutes. Kinsey was a quick learner, and she seemed to grasp the techniques easily. However, she kept getting distracted, with her stomach grumbling audibly.

Sawyer paused, seeing her wince as her stomach growled again. "You really are hungry," he teased. "Must be all last night's exercise."

Kinsey nodded, looking a little embarrassed. "Yeah."

Sawyer frowned, feeling guilty for not taking better care of her. "I'm sorry. We'll have breakfast after this, I promise, but you need to be able to move lightly in case something happens. It's better to be hungry and alert than full and slow."

Kinsey sighed but nodded in agreement. "Okay, you're right. Let's keep going."

They resumed their practice, but Sawyer could see Kinsey getting tired. He decided to call it quits for the morning. They made their way to the kitchen, where Cooper was already brewing a pot of coffee. He grunted in greeting but didn't say much else as he handed them both a mug.

Sawyer could sense the tension in the air as they ate breakfast. Cooper was more taciturn than usual, and his usual gruff demeanor seemed even more severe. Kinsey looked a little uncomfortable, but Sawyer could tell she was trying her best to be polite.

Cooper didn't say much during breakfast, but he did make a mean plate of scrambled eggs and bacon. Sawyer was grateful for the food and the chance to sit down with Kinsey and Cooper and discuss their plans for fortifying the ranch.

"Mike and Viper will be here in a few hours," said Cooper, breaking the silence. "We can start working on the defenses now and finish with them."

Sawyer nodded in agreement. "Good idea. I was thinking we could start with the perimeter fence. We could reinforce it with some steel poles and maybe add some razor wire."

Cooper grunted in approval. "That's a good start. We'll also need to reinforce the windows and doors, and we should make sure we have enough supplies to last us for a while in case we end up in a siege."

Sawyer nodded, happy they were on the same page. "Agreed. We should also have a plan in case Jake shows up. We need to know what we're going to do with him."

Kinsey cleared her throat, stunning Sawyer with her next words. "About that...I think we should guarantee he shows up here, once we're ready. It's a good place to confront him, and I refuse to spend my life running from his sick obsession."

Sawyer's eyes widened in surprise at Kinsey's suggestion. "Are you crazy? We can't just invite him here. It's too dangerous."

Kinsey shook her head, her voice firm. "I know it sounds crazy, but I don't want to spend the rest of my life looking over my shoulder. We need to face him head-on and put an end to this once and for all."

Cooper nodded in agreement, surprising Sawyer. "She's right. We can't keep running forever. If we're going to do this, we need to be prepared and have a plan in place."

Sawyer sighed, knowing he wasn't going to win this argument. "Okay, fine. What's your plan?"

Kinsey took a deep breath. "I want to put the battery back in my phone and let him track me. We'll be prepared for him when he shows up."

Sawyer shook his head in disbelief. "That's crazy. He could come after us at any time."

"But if we're ready for him, we'll have the upper hand," insisted Kinsey.

Cooper nodded in agreement. "She's right. We'll be ready for him. We'll have the element of surprise."

Sawyer sighed, feeling like he was outnumbered. "Okay, fine, but we need to be careful. We don't know what he's capable of."

Kinsey nodded in agreement, and they continued their discussion over breakfast, planning for the worst and hoping for the best.

The three of them worked tirelessly on fortifications for the rest of the morning, making progress on the perimeter fence and reinforcing the windows and doors. As they were taking a quick break for lunch, they heard a car pulling up outside.

Sawyer peeked out the window and saw Viper and Mike getting out of a rented Jeep. He could see the scars on Viper's face even from a distance, and Mike was walking with a slight limp.

He quickly opened the door to let them in, and they exchanged brief greetings before getting to work on the fortifications. Viper moved quickly and efficiently, but his wounds were more internal than external, save for the scars on his face and torso.

Mike, on the other hand, seemed to be struggling a bit. Sawyer could see the pain in his eyes as he walked, but he didn't say anything, not wanting to draw attention to it. Mike was tough and would push through the pain, and he wouldn't appreciate any fussing.

Together, the five of them worked on fortifying the ranch, and by the end of the day, they had made significant progress. As they sat down for dinner, Sawyer was grateful for the support of his friends. "Thanks for coming out here," he said, looking around at the group. "I know it's a long way to travel, and I appreciate it."

Viper shrugged. "You're one of us. We look out for our own."

Mike nodded in agreement, wincing slightly as he shifted in his seat. "We had a pretty flight attendant who made the travel more pleasant." He grinned.

As they ate, they discussed their plans for confronting Jake, with Kinsey insisting on her idea of putting the battery back in her phone and letting him track her. Sawyer still thought it was a crazy idea, as did Mike, but Cooper and Viper were supportive.

They worked out the details and made a plan. Then they played a few hands of cards, where Kinsey displayed an unknown talent for calling their bluffs, before breaking up for the night.

Later, as they laid in bed, Sawyer's thoughts were consumed with the upcoming confrontation with Jake. He turned to Kinsey. "Are you sure about this plan? It's risky. We don't know what Jake will do."

"I know we're taking a big risk by confronting Jake, but I can't continue to live like this."

He sighed and nodded. In that case, we'll do everything we can to make sure you're safe, but we need to be prepared for the worst."

Kinsey nodded. "I know, but I have all of you here to protect me."

Sawyer felt a lump form in his throat as he looked at her. He had grown incredibly attached to Kinsey in a short amount of time. He didn't want to let her go, even when this was all over. "Kinsey, I'm not going to let anything happen to you. I'll do whatever it takes to keep you safe."

Kinsey turned to him, her eyes softening. "I know," she said, reaching out to take his hand. "I trust you, Sawyer. You've already done so much for me."

Warmth spread through his chest at her words. He would do whatever it took to protect her, even if it meant putting himself in danger, and he treasured the trust she showed in him. "I don't want to let you go. "When this is all over, I mean. I don't want to say goodbye."

Kinsey smiled at him with a soft expression. "You won't have to. I don't want to say goodbye either."

Sawyer reached up to brush a curl from her face, breathing a deep sigh of relief. "Good." He leaned in to kiss her gently. "I don't plan on going anywhere." Sawyer's mind drifted to the upcoming confrontation with Jake, and he felt a surge of fear and anger bubble up inside him. "Promise me something," he said suddenly, breaking the silence.

Kinsey looked at him curiously. "What's that?"

"That you'll listen to me and the others if we give you a command," he said, his voice firm. "No matter what happens, I need to know you'll be safe, and like it or not, we know a lot more about how to do that than you do."

Kinsey's expression softened, and she reached out to take his hand. "I promise, but you have to promise me something too."

Sawyer raised an eyebrow. "What's that?"

"That you'll come back to me," she said, her voice barely above a whisper. "No matter what happens, you have to come back to me."

Sawyer felt a lump form in his throat, and he nodded. "I promise." He couldn't truly make that promise, but he refused to admit that, and she apparently didn't want to think about reality either, because she breathed a deep sigh and cuddled closer when he said, "I'll always come back to you."

Chapter 9

KINSEY WOKE EARLY THE next morning, feeling refreshed and energized. They had a long day of fortifications ahead, so she decided to make breakfast for everyone. She quietly slipped out of bed and made her way to the kitchen.

As she gathered ingredients and utensils, she heard someone enter the room. She turned to see Viper, his scarred face looking serious but welcoming. "Hey," he said, his voice low. "Mind some company?"

Kinsey smiled, feeling grateful for the company. "Of course not," she said, gesturing for him to join her. "I'm making breakfast for everyone."

Viper nodded, pulling up a stool next to her. They worked in companionable silence for a few minutes, Kinsey feeling a little nervous around the imposing figure of the former soldier. As they worked together, she found herself opening up to him about her life and her experiences.

Viper listened intently, nodding in understanding as she talked about Jake and everything that had happened. When she finished, he said, "Sawyer's always been that way. He's always been driven to protect people, even before we were in the military."

Kinsey looked at him curiously. "What do you mean?"

Viper shrugged. "It's hard to explain. But even as a boy, Sawyer had this instinct to watch out for others. He always put everyone else's safety above his own."

Warmth spread through her chest as she felt even more drawn to Sawyer than before. "That's amazing," she said, smiling at Viper.

He nodded in agreement before standing up. "I should go join the others on patrol."

As Viper left, Kinsey was grateful for the men who were willing to protect her, even if was because of loyalty to Sawyer, not her. When Sawyer and Cooper walked in, looking tired but determined, she was proud to be part of their team, even if her contribution was something as small as breakfast.

Together, they all sat down to a hearty breakfast of eggs, bacon, and toast. They discussed their plans for the day, and Viper and Cooper headed out on morning patrol while Sawyer and Mike stayed behind to work on the fortifications with Kinsey.

Kinsey spent the morning working alongside Sawyer and Mike to reinforce the fence around the ranch. Sawyer was in charge of the heavy work, using his strength on the manual post-hole digger to force steel poles into the ground. Kinsey watched in awe as he worked, his muscles flexing with each movement.

Meanwhile, she and Mike worked on attaching the razor wire to the poles, carefully weaving it through and securing it in place. As they worked, Kinsey noticed how easily Sawyer slipped into his role as protector. He kept a watchful eye on the perimeter, always alert for any signs of danger. Kinsey admired his determination and bravery, and she felt safe with him by her side.

Mike told stories from their time in the military, making them laugh and easing the tension of the situation. "Hey, Sawyer, remember that time in Afghanistan when we were on patrol, and you got so spooked by that goat that you nearly shot it?" Mike chuckled, looking over at Sawyer.

Sawyer rolled his eyes but grinned. "Yeah, yeah. You don't have to remind me."

Kinsey laughed, enjoying the camaraderie between the two men. "What happened?"

Mike grinned, clearly enjoying the opportunity to embarrass Sawyer. "It kept charging him and tried to pee on him. Sawyer nearly shot the damn thing, but I managed to talk him down before he did any damage."

Sawyer shook his head, but a small smile played on his lips. "I wasn't spooked by the goat. I was just on edge from all the activity in the area."

Kinsey smiled, enjoying the light-hearted banter. "Did the goat pee on you?"

"Just a bit on my boot," said Sawyer with a wince, indicating it was still a sore point. He wiped the sweat from his forehead, his muscles straining as he lifted a heavy pole into place.

"Hey, Mike, tell us another story," she said, hoping to distract herself from drudgery of the task at hand.

Mike chuckled, leaning against the fence. "Well, there was this one time in Kabul when we were on a mission to take out some insurgents. We were holed up in this abandoned building, and I swear, every time we tried to make a move, something would go wrong."

Sawyer groaned, looking at Mike. "Not when we got stuck waiting?"

Mike grinned, his eyes sparkling. "You know me too well, brother. That's the story indeed." He looked back at Kinsey. "We were stuck in this room for hours, waiting for the right moment to strike, and Sawyer had to take a pi..." He cleared his throat. "Well, he went and did his business, and we had to move in the meantime, so he came back with his pants around his thighs, his expression stone-cold even as his johnson slipped from his shorts to salute the insurgents."

Kinsey laughed as Sawyer shook his head and drove the post into the ground more forcefully than necessary. "Why don't you tell her some embarrassing stories about you?"

"Nah, where's the fun in that?" asked Mike with an unrepentant grin.

As they worked, they continued to share stories, and Kinsey found herself feeling more and more at ease with the men. They were tough and resilient, but they also had a sense of humor and deep camaraderie.

The hours passed quickly, and soon they had almost everything completed. They were finishing up when Cooper and Viper returned in Cooper's old farm truck. Lex sat up front between them, looking proud, and when the door opened, Scooter jumped off Vipers lap and to the ground to start barking at Viper and Kinsey. She grinned and held out a hand, speaking softly. He gave her a suspicious look but circled around her and went into the house.

As she turned to face the men who'd been all over the sprawling property, she couldn't miss the exhaustion etched into Viper and Cooper's faces, though they still looked determined.

Between Mike's stories and their clear perseverance, she had an even deeper respect for the men who had served their country, putting their lives on the line for others.

Kinsey worked alongside Mike and Sawyer as they prepared dinner. Mike was grilling steaks and veggies while Kinsey made side salads. Cooper had thrown together strawberry shortcake with homemade biscuits for dessert. It felt like a family feast, but it also had an eerie undertone of a last meal.

As they worked, the men made small talk, joking and laughing with each other. They included Kinsey in their conversations, making her feel like she was part of the group.

"So, Kinsey, tell us about your life before all this," said Mike, flipping a steak on the grill.

Kinsey smiled, feeling a little self-conscious about sharing her story. "I grew up in a shitty New Jersey town with a single mom who worked three jobs. She was always working, and when she was infrequently at home, she was usually criticizing me for something."

Sawyer and Cooper exchanged a sympathetic look, and Mike frowned in understanding. "That sounds tough."

Kinsey nodded as a lump formed in her throat. "Yeah, it was, but things got worse when my mom's last boyfriend got handsy with me. I left at seventeen, came to New York City like a moron, and have been working as a waitress ever since while struggling to make rent—until I met Jake. I think part of why he swept me off my feet so quickly was because he seemed to care about me and want to protect me. I see now he didn't though." She put her hand on Sawyer's. "A real man showed me what that really means."

The men fell silent, their faces full of sympathy and understanding. Kinsey appreciated their support, feeling a sense of camaraderie with them.

As they finished preparing dinner, Kinsey couldn't shake the feeling of unease. They were ready to confront Jake, but she couldn't help but wonder if they were truly prepared for what could happen. Finally, she spoke up. "Do you think we're ready to summon Jake?" she asked, her voice low.

Sawyer looked up from his plate, his eyes serious. "We've done everything we can to prepare. We have the fortifications, and we have a plan in case he shows up. We're as ready as we'll ever be."

Kinsey nodded, determination settling over her. She had to confront Jake, no matter how scary it might be. "Should I text one of my friends at the restaurant with my own phone?"

Sawyer shook his head. "Not tonight. We'll put the battery back in your phone tomorrow morning. It's better not to face him at night. We need to be alert and ready for anything."

Kinsey nodded in agreement, relieved they had a tentative plan. "Okay. What do we do when he comes here?"

Sawyer looked at her gravely. "We'll confront him. The guys and I will make sure he knows he can't come after you anymore."

A sense of trepidation settled in her stomach, but they had to do this. She couldn't spend the rest of her life looking over her shoulder, waiting for Jake to show up. At least she had these men to help her. They were a team, and they were in this together. No matter what happened, they would face it as a group.

Chapter 10

SAWYER WOKE UP EARLY the next morning, feeling a sense of anticipation in the air. He and the others had spent the previous day fortifying the ranch, and now it was time to put their plan into action. He looked over at Kinsey, who was already awake and dressed. "Ready?" he asked, sitting up in bed.

Kinsey nodded, her expression determined. "As ready as I'll ever be."

They got dressed and headed to the kitchen, where Cooper and Viper were already eating breakfast. Mike was outside checking the perimeter.

Sawyer and Kinsey joined them, and Cooper passed them plates of eggs and toast. They ate in silence, the tension in the air almost palpable.

When they finished, Sawyer led Kinsey to the living room, where they had left her phone charging overnight. He inserted the battery, and Kinsey turned on the phone. She sent a text message to her friend at the restaurant, telling her she was safe in Texas and giving a vague location of Cooper's ranch while mentioning Cooper's name. They waited for a response from Beth, but none came.

Sawyer's phone rang, and he answered it, his expression serious. He listened for a moment before hanging up. "That was Mike. He just did a perimeter check, and everything looks clear, but we need to be on high alert. Jake could show up any time."

Kinsey nodded, looking nervous but determined. They spent the rest of the day on edge, waiting for any sign of Jake. They kept busy, doing small tasks around the ranch, but they were all on edge.

As the day wore on, and the sun began to set, they all started to feel anxious. They had been waiting for hours, and there was still no sign of Jake. Finally, as the night fell, they decided to call it a day. Sawyer and Kinsey retreated to their room, exhausted but still on edge. Jake could still show up at any moment.

As they laid in bed, Kinsey turned to Sawyer. "What if he doesn't come?" she asked, her voice trembling slightly. She just wanted this to be over.

Sawyer wrapped his arm around her, pulling her close. "He'll come," he said, his voice low and determined. "We just have to be patient. And when he does, we'll be ready."

SAWYER FELL ASLEEP holding Kinsey, but his rest was short-lived. He woke to the sound of a chopper's whirring blades, the noise stirring memories of his time in Afghanistan. He sat up in bed, his heart racing with fear. The sound was so familiar, so distinct, and it filled him with a sense of dread.

He looked over at Kinsey, still fast asleep, and was tempted to leave her sleeping. Maybe they could deal with Jake in moments, and he could tell her about it in the morning. Only knowing she'd be ticked if he did that had him whispering, "Kinsey, wake up. We need to get the others."

She stirred, her eyes bleary with sleep when her lids peeled open. "What's going on?" Her voice was groggy.

Sawyer didn't answer. He just grabbed her hand and pulled her out of bed. They rushed to the living room, where Cooper and Viper were already awake, their expressions alert.

"You hear that?" asked Cooper, his brow furrowed.

Viper nodded, his hand already on his weapon. "Sounds like a chopper."

Sawyer's heart rate increased even more as the sound got louder. They had to act fast. As he struggled to keep his emotions in check, Scooter barked like crazy. Even Lex, who was usually calm and collected, had started to bark.

The men gathered near the front door, doing a last-minute weapons check. He turned to Kinsey when she tried to exit with them. "Stay here."

"But—"

"Remember your promise." He scowled. "You know only basic self-defense and haven't learned how to shoot a rifle. You'll be safer here, and so will we."

"Fine." She seemed unhappy but didn't argue.

He secured his own weapon and motioned for the others to follow him at double-time pace. He led the rush outside, and they all had their weapons at the ready. The sound of the chopper was now deafening, and Sawyer saw it getting closer. Anxiety settled over him, and he knew this was it. This was the moment they had been dreading.

He took a deep breath, trying to steady his nerves. He had a job to do, and he couldn't let his fear get the best of him. He turned to the others and motioned for them to get into position.

The sound of the helicopters grew louder before setting down in the pasture, and figures in black tactical gear disembarked. What kind of budget did Jake have that he could hire mercs?

He signaled for the others to move forward, their weapons trained on the approaching figures. As they crept forward, Sawyer couldn't shake the memories of Afghanistan. The sound of the choppers, the adrenaline coursing through his veins, and the fear and uncertainty of what was to come. It was all too familiar, and he struggled to keep his emotions in check.

As the group approached the figures, Sawyer had to focus. He couldn't let his past experiences cloud his judgment, not when so much was at stake. He motioned for the others to hold their fire, hoping to catch the figures off-guard.

As they stood there, Sawyer's mind raced with thoughts of their plan. Would it work? Would they be able to catch Jake and bring him to justice? They crept forward, their weapons trained on the figures approaching them.

Sawyer's heart was pounding in his chest, and sweat beaded his forehead, but he couldn't let his fear control him. He had to be strong for Kinsey and for the others. They had a job to do, and he was determined to see it through.

As they approached the figures, they were armed and dangerous. "Drop your weapons," he yelled, his voice loud and commanding. "We have you surrounded."

The figures hesitated for a moment, but then one of them made a run for the cover of the barn. Viper fired a warning shot, causing the figure to stop in his tracks. Sawyer moved forward, his weapon trained on the man. "Who are you and what do you want?"

The man didn't answer until Sawyer pressed the rifle into his back, forcing him to his knees. He snugged the barrel against the back of his head. "You're obviously a merc, so who's your employer?"

With a tremble, the man spoke. "I'm part of the first team, here for Kinsey," he said, his voice shaky. "I have a message from Jake."

Sawyer's heart raced. "What does he want?"

"He just wants Kinsey," said the man. "He's willing to pay for her. A lot of money."

Sawyer's blood boiled at the mention of money. Jake was trying to buy his way out of this, but he wasn't going to let that happen.

"We're not interested in money," said Sawyer. "Tell Jake to turn himself in, and we'll consider leniency."

The man hesitated for a moment before he shook his head. "I can't do that. Jake won't go down without a fight."

Sawyer knew what that meant. He signaled to the others, and they moved into position, their weapons at the ready. Before they could take action, Jake and the rest of his goons in tactical gear appeared, firing their weapons. Jake didn't even consider the safety of his own hired guns, who crouched in the pasture after being disarmed.

Sawyer and the others returned fire, ducking behind cover as bullets whizzed past them. His heart pounded as he fired back, determined to protect Kinsey and his team.

The firefight was quick and bloody, but there didn't seem to be any fatalities, and all the casualties were on the mercs' side. Sawyer stood with his friends as they circled around the group moments later, having forced them all to kneel in the pasture. "Where's Jake?"

"I don't know," said Cooper.

"Right here, buddy," said a sinister voice behind him as the muzzle of a Russian-made rifle caressed his temple. "Turn around."

Slowly, he did so, facing the angular little jerk who was so entitled he'd do all this. "You're outnumbered."

"Perhaps, but I have the gun on you. Kinsey, get out here," he shouted, spittle flying.

Sawyer's mind raced as he tried to come up with a plan. He couldn't let Kinsey come out and put herself in danger, but he also couldn't let Jake get away with what he had done. "Don't do it, honey," he called, and the barrel pressed more firmly against his temple.

Suddenly, Kinsey strode toward them, her voice strong and clear, ringing with rage. "Jake, you have no right to treat me this way," she said. "I don't love you, and I don't want to be with you."

Jake's face twisted with anger, and he tightened his grip on the gun. "You belong with me, Kinsey, and you'll come with me, or I'll kill him."

Sawyer had to act fast. He launched himself at Jake, tackling him to the ground and knocking the gun out of his hand. He sent Jake sprawling on the ground as he swung his rifle to keep the pissant from moving. "Part of me wants to tell you to freeze, but part of me hopes you try. So just try it, Jake." There was no artifice in his threatening tone.

As he looked up, he saw Kinsey rushing towards him, a look of concern on her face. Just then, Sawyer heard the sound of another helicopter approaching. Kinsey reached him, and he took her into his arms, swinging her behind him as he turned to face the possible new threat as it landed beside Jake's merc chopper in the pasture.

The debris and dust blew around them, since the second chopper didn't shut down. Two people were sliding out, and as he squinted through the cloud stirred by the chopper, he recognized Major Clayton Johnson disembarking from the chopper.

"Major Johnson," he said, stepping forward to greet him, raising his voice slightly to be heard over the slowly rotating rotors.

The major smiled, his eyes crinkling at the corners. "It's good to see you, Sawyer, and it looks like you've been keeping busy."

Sawyer nodded, still feeling a bit shaky from the recent events. "Yeah, we've had a few things to deal with."

Clayton turned to the man standing next to him. "I'd like you to meet James Howard. He's the CEO of the cybersecurity company where Jake works, and his top-secret tech is how Jake was tracking you."

James looked nervous as he shook hands with Sawyer and the others. "I'm sorry about all this. I had no idea what my son was up to."

Sawyer didn't know if he believed that. "Really. How convenient."

James frowned. "I truly didn't. My wife told me to start him out at the bottom of the company, but I wanted to make it easier on him, so I gave him a cushy executive job right out of high school." He shook his head, clearly now finding that decision foolish.

He looked at Kinsey. "I'm really sorry you've been through this, hon. I wish you'd said something to me or Frannie when we were at your place for Easter."

Kinsey swayed before nodding. "I didn't know if you'd help me. He said you knew everything he was doing."

James snorted. "Nope, and I sure wouldn't risk my company or DOD contracts for this foolishness."

"What are you going to do to him?" asked Sawyer.

"If James hadn't cooperated, we would have cancelled his DOD contracts and investigated him. As it is, we're investigating Jake," said Clayton.

He nodded his approval. "I was talking to Mr. Howard though."

James sighed heavily. "I'm going to have him transferred to our manufacturing division in Europe unless he has to stand trial here. He'll be working in the mail room. It's the least I can do to try and make things right."

Jake whimpered. "You can't do that, Dad. I'm much better than that."

"Clearly you aren't." His father looked enraged. "Don't you dare take a superior attitude after what you've done. I might even start you on the cleaning crew at this point if you don't shut up."

Jake bent his head, sending a sulky glare at his father and Kinsey, but he didn't say anything else.

Sawyer nodded slowly after exchanging a glance with Kinsey. It wasn't justice in the traditional sense, but at least Jake wouldn't be able to hurt anyone else. If he didn't stand trial on charges from the military or government, he'd be much more closely monitored either way.

James and Clayton quickly moved to apprehend Jake and dragged him away.

As they left with Jake between them, Clayton gestured to men in black tac gear spilling from the chopper, who clearly had government ties. They began to round up the mercenaries that Jake had hired, reading them their rights and placing them under arrest as one of them called for a paddy wagon.

Sawyer was relieved as he watched the whole group go more than an hour later. Kinsey was still at his side, leaning against him, and he felt her sigh. It was finally over. Jake was in custody, and they had put an end to his illegal activities.

He turned to Kinsey, who looked dazed. "Come on. Let's go inside."

Inside the house, Sawyer helped Kinsey to the couch, where she sat down heavily. He could see the exhaustion and shock written on her face.

"You okay?" he asked, sitting down beside her.

She nodded, but her voice was barely above a whisper. "I just can't believe it's over."

Sawyer put an arm around her, holding her close. "It's over," he said, his voice soft. "We did it." As Kinsey and Sawyer hugged each other tightly, the other men started to filter back into the house.

After a few minutes, Cooper spoke up. "So, what now?"

Sawyer looked at Kinsey, then back at Cooper. "I don't know. What do you guys think?"

Cooper rubbed his chin thoughtfully. "Well, we've got plenty of space here. If you guys want, you can stay here for a while. Get your bearings and figure out your next move. If your bar can spare you."

Sawyer snorted, admitting what he'd been ignoring for a while. "I can't afford to keep it open. Not enough clientele."

Kinsey smiled gratefully even as she patted Sawyer's hand in a consoling fashion. "That's really kind of you, Cooper. Thank you."

Sawyer nodded in agreement. "Yeah, we appreciate it. We could use some time away from the city, that's for sure."

Viper said, "I think I'm going to head back to Chicago. I've got some loose ends to tie up there."

Mike was silent for a moment before he said, "I'll think about it, and I might take you up on that offer, Cooper. I could use a change of scenery."

Cooper grinned. "You're welcome here any time, Mike. We're like family, after all."

Sawyer was grateful, and a lump formed in his throat. These disparate guys were his brothers in every way that counted, and he and Kinsey were lucky to have them in their lives.

Epilogue

A FEW WEEKS LATER, Kinsey sat on the porch, looking out over the vast expanse of land that stretched out before her. The sun was just beginning to set, casting a warm glow over everything in its path. She couldn't believe how much her life had changed in just a few short weeks.

Sawyer came up behind her, wrapping his arms around her waist. She leaned back against him, feeling safe and loved. "What are you thinking about?" he asked, his voice low and gentle.

Kinsey turned to face him, smiling. "I was just thinking how much I love it here. I don't think I want to go back to New York City."

Sawyer raised an eyebrow, surprised. "Really? I thought you loved the city."

"I did once upon a time, when I was first there, before I had to work so much and have five roommates." She shrugged. "Now...I don't. Being out here, surrounded by nature, just feels so right."

Sawyer smiled, pulling her closer. "I know what you mean. I feel the same way. I've had an offer on the building, so I plan to sell it if you don't want to go back. I want to be where you are."

Happiness filled her as she looked up into his eyes. Without a doubt, she wanted to spend the rest of her life with him. "You don't want to go back?"

"No. It's just another broken dream, and I'm ready to put all that behind me, but if we're going to stay here, we should think about buying our own land."

Kinsey's heart leapt at the idea. "Yes, I've been thinking about that too. Maybe we could buy land near Cooper's ranch. It would be a good place to raise a family."

Sawyer's eyes widened. "A family?"

And then, before she could even think about it, the words just spilled out. "I'm pregnant."

Sawyer's eyes widened in surprise, but then he grinned. "That's amazing," he said, pulling her close again. "I can't wait to be a dad."

They stood there for a few moments, just enjoying the moment, until Sawyer got down on one knee, removing a ring from his pocket. "I bought this during the last trip to Abilene, but I didn't want to rush you. We've only been together for a short time, but I want to spend the rest of my life with you. Will you marry me?"

Tears filled Kinsey's eyes as she nodded, her heart overflowing with joy. "Yes," she said, her voice barely above a whisper as she held out her left hand. "I love you."

Sawyer slipped the ring on her finger, and they held each other closely, watching as the sun sank below the horizon. They had no idea what the future might hold, but they would face it together. They had been through so much in such a short time, but they had come out of it stronger than ever before.

She was ready to face whatever challenges lay ahead as long as they were together. As the sun set behind them, they shared a kiss, their hearts filled with love and hope for the future. She was thrilled to have found someone so special and would do whatever it took to hold onto him. She didn't have to wonder if he had the same commitment, because she already knew he'd fight for her.

Together, they walked back into Cooper's house, ready to start the next chapter of their lives as husband and wife, just as soon as they could plan a wedding. Then, the next step would be Mommy and Daddy, which made her shiver with delight and a little fear, though she wasn't truly afraid. They would tackle parenthood together, just like everything else.

About Mia

THANK YOU FOR READING! I hope you enjoyed reading this book as much as I loved writing it!

If so, you might be interested in my reader club, where you'll get notice of new releases, specials, and other great goodies (like FREE books and FREE Chapters of upcoming releases).

As a special thank you, **you'll immediately get my book The Boardroom Connection, for FREE when you sign up**. No strings, you can unsubscribe anytime, and I promise I won't blow up your inbox.

What do you think?

YES – I'm in! I want to know the moment you drop a new release and get my FREE book! [Add Link: https://dl.bookfunnel.com/g14g65dcmd]

No, that's alright. I get enough emails, and I'll keep up with your new releases another way.

Again, I hope you enjoyed this book. You can learn more about my newest releases here: https://bwwmlovestories.com/latest-releases/mia-latest/[1]

---

1.   https://l.facebook.com/

l.php?u=https%3A%2F%2Fbwwmlovestories.com%2Flatest-releases%2Fmia-latest%2F%3Ffbclid%3DIwZXh0bgNhZW0CMTAAAR34HFLR7qBe4ZmBHns_e

4d0XgNzeLpuTKitrQtc8gfqYam6Jwke4d05P5M_aem_AXZgxaooVqdkRI8v5k6ceTy

7Gin_SGSOwZ0mohUpkMmzR-

Suzibzrob5LkW28qL53CXma0uvn_jG_N2FBJWICaiR&h=AT0CMUeqAaRQCxB

And if you get a chance to drop a review or rating, I'd really appreciate it.

Best,

Mia

---

vibJCLOB3BJo5qSFoE64VilifGretJ6ZtzkQOn3BhZ4e4cTX1Dpuw0RpYrElXkhsQl qHZNi1DZdWlWOBOS2jn6YcuV5YinE0EhazJOy56rM3zQC4ziRiIOHCHTe8ohj 45g&__tn__=-UK-
R&c%5b0%5d=AT06pfvEYO5wdSYGkilnE_RlU_XJQ3YtaKVXM3kw2RVJU7AE HMWZrKbz4ZVZ5KpHSvCa7Rpb3D9k4_NQuxDrhwHZHAVAvzrcdwCUjfoVu Au6L2M3OoNNZ9qa849xyadSBygYxrAoFCijWjBix80lUGrim2l7h4DWuGnd8vR M3D-hcJAbp-sg41WLy5X32P7Q

About Mylia

IF YOU WOULD LIKE TO be the first to hear about new releases, please join my mailing list[1] and receive a free book. I love to hear from readers, so please feel free to email me at authormashton@yahoo.com.

---

1. https://subscribeto.eo.page/myliaashton